Published in Great Britain by Canongate Press, April 1992
Published on the same day in the United States by
    Pelican Publishing Company, Inc., April 1992

ISBN 0-88289-928-7

Library of Congress Catalog Card Number: 92-70410

Manufactured in Great Britain
Published by Pelican Publishing Company, Inc.
1101 Monroe Street, Gretna, Louisiana 70053

VENUS PETER
SAVES THE WHALE

Christopher Rush

Illustrated by

Mairi Hedderwick

PELICAN PUBLISHING COMPANY
Gretna 1992

Venus Peter woke up to a morning that was loud with seagulls. He had been dreaming deeply about sailing on his grandfather's boat but the noise of the seabirds broke into his dream and cracked it open like an egg.

"Come on out, Peter!" they were screeching. "Come on, Venus Peter, it's time you were up!"

Peter tried to open his eyes but his eyelids were stuck down with sandman's glue so he opened his ears wider instead. He could hear his mother taking in the porridge to old Epp, his great-aunt.

"What a racket the gulls are making this morning," his mother was saying.

"It's a wonder they don't waken that boy of yours," he heard Epp reply.

Then the gulls broke out again even louder this time: "Venus Peter, Venus Peter, it's a fine fishing morning! Hurry up, or you'll miss the best of the day!"

Suddenly there was a loud shriek very close at hand.

"Get yourself out of bed, boy," the screeching said. "There's a big catch out there today. You'd better not miss the tide!"

Peter heaved the window up and jumped straight out among the strawberries. A huge gull was perched on the rim of the chimney pot, screaming downwards, its big yellow eye peering sideways into the blackness. Peter popped a gigantic strawberry onto his tongue.

"I'm here," he said, through a mouthful of bright red juice.

"Oh, there you are," chattered the seagull in a quieter voice. "I thought maybe you couldn't hear me for sleep!"

"What's all the noise about?" asked Peter.

"Are you blind as well as deaf?" the seagull squawked. "Look up in the sky."

The big-beaked bird rose from the roof, spreading its white wings wide. Shading his eyes from the sun, Peter followed the path it took through the blue morning. Out beyond the breakwater all the gulls for miles around had flocked together and had arranged themselves into three great big words, high above the harbour. Peter screwed his eyes up tight and read their message:

THAR SHE BLOWS!

That means there's a whale, thought Peter excitedly, but though he searched the sea from east to west and scanned the horizon carefully, he could see no sign of a waterspout.

There IS a whale, Venus Peter!

Guthrie BAKER

Just then there came the sound of hooves clattering up the steep brae and the baker's cart jolted to a stop at the garden gate.

"Hey, Mr Guthrie!" yelled Peter. "Can you see a whale from up there?"

From his high seat behind the horse Mr Guthrie roared, and laughed, "Bless you, no, I can't, my boy, but I can see your grandad's curtains are still drawn. If he doesn't get up soon the *Venus* will be the last boat out of harbour. The crew are down there raring to go!"

And with an expert swing of his arm he threw Peter the paper poke containing a dozen rolls. It landed with a floury thump on the flagstones at his feet.

Peter snatched it up and dived back into the house through the open window. Then he chugged up the stairs as noisily as a steam train, with wispy puffs of flour trailing behind him from the burst bag.

Not bothering to knock, he ran straight into his grandparents' bedroom and pulled back the blankets from the old folks' bed.

Grandfather was lying stretched out in his long johns, his white hairy vest buttoned up to the neck. He was like a sleeping snowman, missing only his pipe and his cap. Grandmother lay at his side like a snowman's wife in her huge long nightgown with its masses of embroidery and lace.

"Grandad!" shouted Peter. "It's high time you were up!"

Neither of them moved. Peter dropped the bag of rolls on the floor and grabbed his grandparents' blankets with both hands, shaking them furiously. Grandfather stirred, making sea noises and grandmother's nightgown rippled like a sail captured by the wind. Peter was fascinated. He shook the blankets harder and the nightgown flapped and billowed furiously.

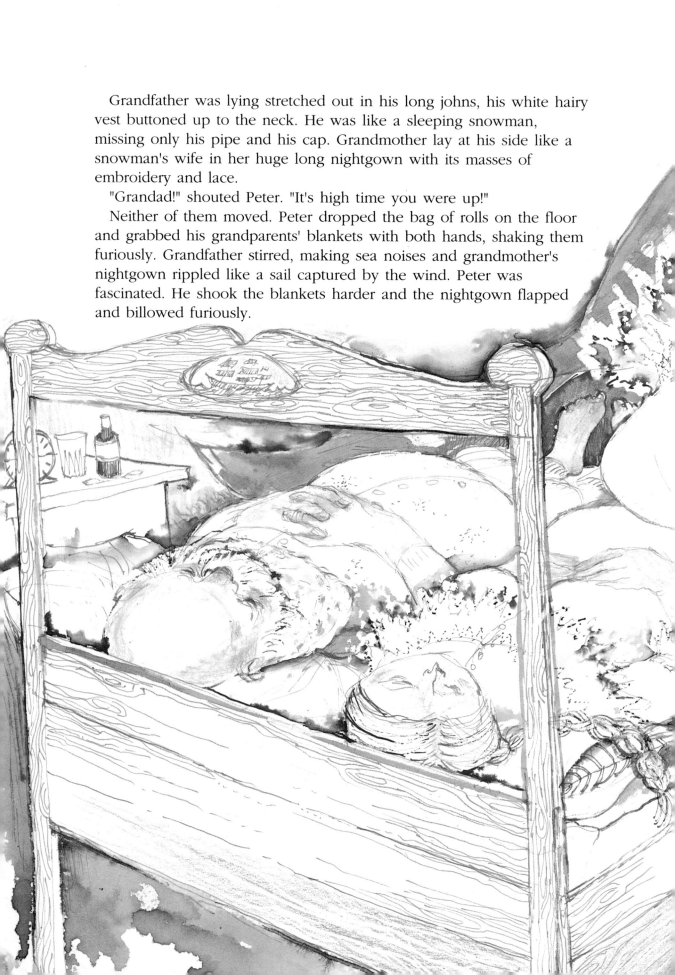

Tickle their toes!

"The baker's been, grandad. He says you'll be the last out of port and the crew are all waiting for you. And there's a whale out there too!"

Peter shouted the words through the old man's beard to reach his ears. There were still some sticky seeds clinging to his whiskers, left over from yesterday's walk in the woods. Peter stood back from the bed among the scattered rolls and gave a big salute.

"Ready to set sail, grandad?"

At last his grandparents stretched themselves, yawned and sat up.

"You young rascal, what have you been doing with the rolls?" wailed grandmother. "Your great-aunt Epp will go daft if there's flour on her floors!"

But grandfather just walked to the window, flung back the curtains and smiled.

"You're right, lad," he said, "it's a fine morning for the whales – though I think I'll make do with the herring."

He started pulling on his clothes.

"Give me a roll from the bag, Peter. I'll just eat one on the way." And he took his cap from behind the door and shouted cheerio to everybody in the house.

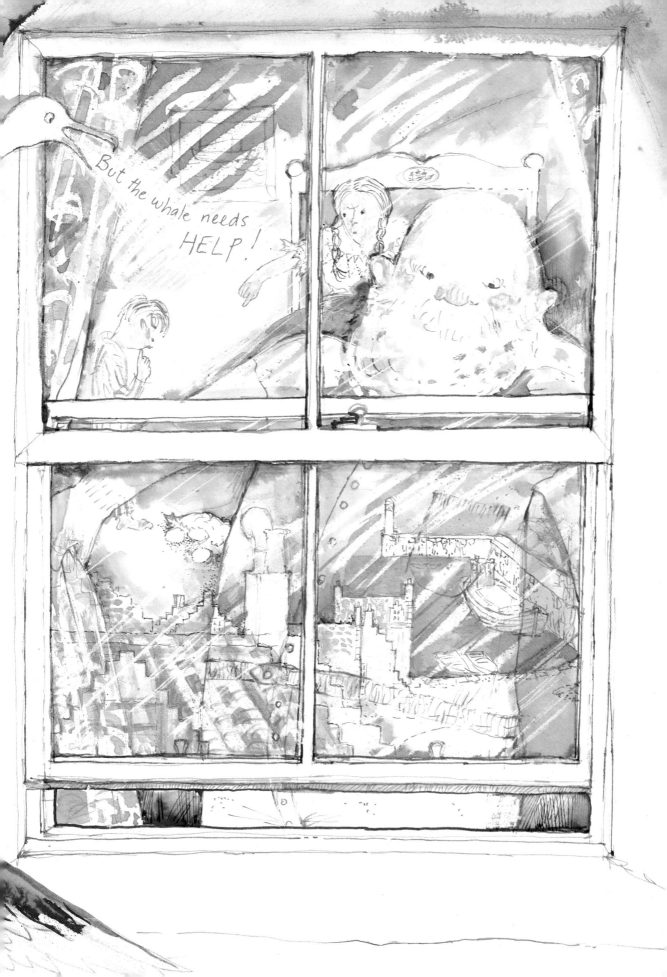

"I'd better find out about this whale," Peter said to himself, and he ran back downstairs and into the garden, still in his pyjamas.

By this time the seagull on the roof was going frantic.

"What's keeping you?" it skirled at Peter.

"Nothing! I'm coming," he panted, running down the path.

"Peter! Come back here at once, you haven't had your breakfast!" It was his mother's voice.

Peter paused by the bottom of the strawberry patch to cram another of the jumbo-sized berries into his mouth.

That's it, Venus Peter!
Keep going! On past
the church!

"That'll do me, mum. Sorry – important message – I won't be long."

He ran past his grandfather all the way down the brae, shedding his slippers as he went. Three boats were still in the harbour getting up steam, the *Dawn*, the *Acorn*, and the *Venus* which was skippered by his grandfather.

Peter bellowed across the harbour.

"My grandad's just coming . . . Have any of you seen a whale?"

"Not in the last wee while!" shouted the cook, waving back at him, and the whole crew rocked the *Venus* with their laughter.

So Peter ran on, past the boatbuilder's yard, past the last houses, down the steps and over the bridge till he came to the church – but still no whale. Instead he saw a white thundercloud of seabirds hovering above the clifftop just beyond the churchyard. He raced along the rocks, jumping from boulder to boulder (all his favourite ones) until finally, rounding the corner of the cliff and coming to the little beach, he saw with a shock what all the fuss had been about.

Yes, there was a whale after all – and a whacking great whale it was! And it was green! Greater and greener than a great big hill, studded with starfish and sea-shells like daisies growing on its back.

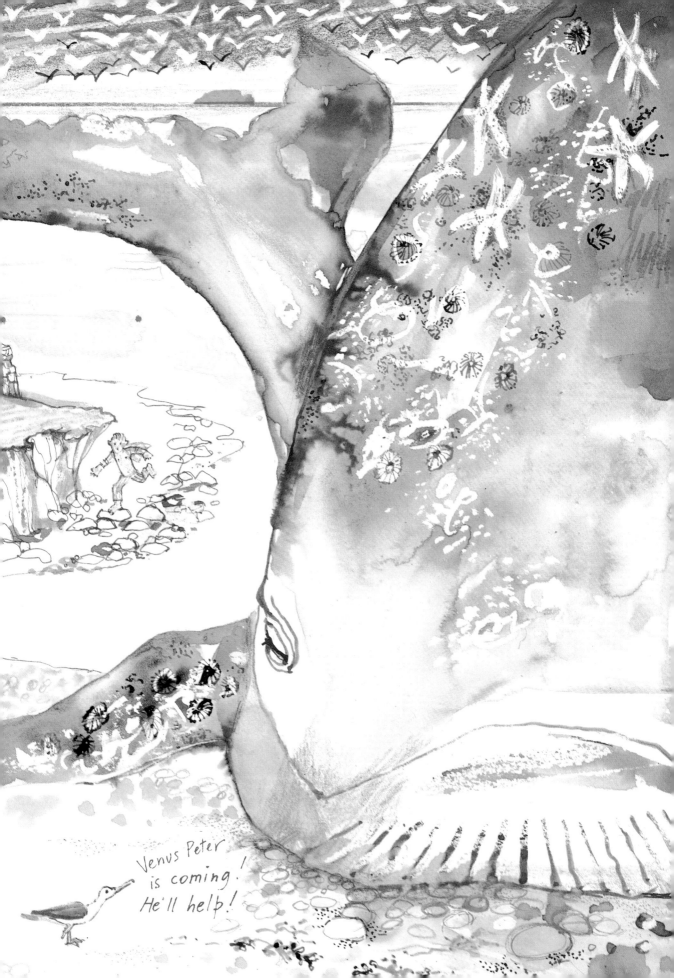

Venus Peter
is coming!
He'll help!

Don't worry, his grandfather has a boat...

The great sea-beast lay stranded on the sand. It couldn't move an inch.
But it could manage a whisper, even though it was out of the water.

"Help at last," it breathed. "I thought you were never coming, and
I'm in real trouble, as you can see. If I stay here much longer I'm sure
to die."

"But how can I help?" asked Peter, feeling very small as he stood
there in his bare feet before the biggest thing in the sea.

"Easy," said the whale, "find someone to give me a tow."

How!

MILLER'S
BOATYARD

At that moment Peter saw two boats edging past the breakwater.
"Oh, no!" he cried. "I'm too late!"
The *Acorn* and the *Dawn* had now left the harbour. The *Venus*
would not be far behind. It was too late to save the whale.
Then Peter had an idea,
"Quick!" he yelled to the fluttering gulls. "Stop the *Venus*!"
"How? how? how?" they all wailed together.
"You'll think of something!" shouted Peter, setting off for the harbour
with every seabird in the sky soaring ahead of him.
"I'll be back!" he promised to the whale over his shoulder.
"I'm not going anywhere," winked the whale.

When Peter reached the harbour he found the astonished crew of the *Venus* standing in the stern scratching their heads. Just as the boat had set off half the seagulls had snatched up the mooring rope in their beaks and looped it round the Post Office chimney at the head of the pier. The postmaster was standing waving his hat to the fisherman.

"Don't set sail, lads!" he howled. "You'll bring my chimneys down!"

The rest of the birds had blocked up the *Venus's* wheelhouse. She could simply not leave harbour.

"It's all right, grandad," called Peter, running along the cobbled pier, "I can explain everything."

And so he did.

POST OFFICE

Half an hour later Peter and the whale were deep in conversation while grandfather's crew were busy tying ropes to its vast tail. The *Venus* was bobbing on the waves just offshore, ready to tow the beast back into the sea.

"That was very clever of you," the whale whispered, "and very kind. What's your name?"

"Peter. What's yours?"

"Joshua," said the whale, squirming a little, "but you can call me Josh, for short. What age are you?"

"Nearly seven," Peter answered. "How old are you?"

"I've lost count," the whale replied. "I can remember men with eagles on their flags, and men with horns on their helmets, and men in big iron whales under the water. I can even remember them on top of the water, shooting harpoons at me."

"I think you must be very old, as old as the earth," said Peter. "Don't you remember any men *without* weapons, any nice men?"

"Not really."

Then the whale's eye brightened.

"But I'll remember you – and the crew of the *Venus*. Oops, here we go, I think. Cheerio, Peter, and thank you – for saving an old whale."

WE'LL MEET AGAIN!   VENUS PETER SAVED THE WHALE!

GOODBYE and THANKYOU!

Then the Venus's engine roared into life. As she hauled on the ropes Joshua slid into the waves, causing a tremendous wash all across the water.

Far out at sea, the *Venus* undid the ropes and grandfather blew three loud toots on the horn specially for Peter. Then he sailed off down the firth towards the North Sea.

The whale swam south.

But before it did so, it said a final farewell. Standing waving from the clifftop, Peter saw three fantastic fountains of water rising out of the sea, one after the other. And this is what they said:

GOODBYE AND THANK YOU!
WE'LL MEET AGAIN!
VENUS PETER SAVED THE WHALE!

I told you he would!